D0230917

GREAT BUNNY BAKES

NEW TURBO SETTING

PUBLISHED TODAY

HOW TO SPOT A WOLF

FREE TOY!

FOR:
Mum,
Grandma Clare
& Nana Ruth.

WHOSE BAKES INSPIRED THIS BOOK

BAKE SALE!

ALL PROCEEDS GO TO CARROT AID

WANTED
CAKE THIEF

REWARD

MISSING

MRS HOP'S LAST CUPCAKE. LAST SEEN FRIDAY AT 4PM.

Carr~o~lite

Made with :REAL: Carrots
HEALTHIER THAN BUTTER!

SAVE OUR BEES

Clara's Cakes

CAKE ACADEMY

PECKSWORTH FARM

EGGS

FRESH

HOMEMADE

SIMON & SCHUSTER
First published in Great Britain in 2018 by Simon & Schuster UK Ltd 1st Floor, 222 Gray's Inn Road, London WC1X 8HB • A CBS Company • Text and illustrations copyright © 2018 Ellie Snowdon • The right of Ellie Snowdon to be identified as the author and illustrator of this work has been asserted by her in accordance with the Copyright, Designs and Patents Act, 1988 All rights reserved, including the right of reproduction in whole or in part in any form • A CIP catalogue record for this book is available from the British Library upon request • ISBN: 978-1-4711-6635-8 (HB) ISBN: 978-1-4711-6634-1 (PB) ISBN: 978-1-4711-6636-5 (eBook) Printed in Italy • 10 9 8 7 6 5 4 3 2 1

GREAT BUNNY BAKES

ELLIE SNOWDON

SIMON & SCHUSTER

London New York Sydney Toronto New Delhi

Quentin was a wolf with an unusual talent.

He LOVED to bake!

Cinnamon buns, crumbly shortbread biscuits,
fondant fancies and his favourite –
chocolate cake.
Quentin loved them all!

But there was one problem.

He had no one to share them with.

Then one day,
a letter arrived.

Quentin was so excited.
But there must have
been a mix-up.

Quentin was a wolf.

How could he enter a competition for bunnies?

Unless . . .

. . . he became a master of disguise!

Quentin looked up and down the queue.
He seemed to blend in perfectly.

Phew!

Just then the judges read out the rules.

'There are *five* challenges in the bunny bake-off and you must complete them all.

The bunny with the most Brownie Points wins.

LET THE BUNNY BAKE-OFF BEGIN!'

BREAD

First up, was the Bread round.
Every baker needed to be able to bake the perfect loaf!

The dough proved to be a bit of a nightmare
for some of the bakers.

But not for Quentin.

He wanted to show everyone
what he could do.

'Ooh! Lovely!' said one judge.

'Ten points!' cried the other.

Next, the contestants needed to wobble their way
to the top with their best trifles!

Quentin's trifle scored the biggest wobble on the wobble-o-meter anyone had ever seen.

'Incredible!'

'Look at that wobble!' cried the judges.

Things were going rather well.

Honey Buns

For the third challenge, the bakers were asked
to build a tall tower of Honey Buns.

Everything was a *hive* of activity until . . . .

Someone let the bees in!

OUCH!

But a few bees wouldn't stop Quentin.
His Honey Bun tower stretched sky-high!

The judges were very impressed.

(And the bees were too!)

PASTRY PIE

For the fourth round, the bakers had to
stay humble and make the most perfect pastry pie.

But something very odd was going on.

Quentin's berry pie didn't taste nice at all.
It was VERY salty.

The judges agreed.

Quentin was just trying to work out
what had happened when . . .

. . . it turned out that one contestant was no *cutie pie!*

NAUGHTINESS WILL NOT BE TOLERATED

PLEASE WASH-UP (FOR EXTRA BROWNIE POINTS)

SPOONS

TINS

He had swapped Quentin's sugar for salt!

What a dirty trick.
And definitely against the rules.

STAGE DOOR

BOO!

CHOCOLATE CAKE EXTRAVAGANZA!

At last it was time for the final round and
the ultimate challenge –
the CHOCOLATE CAKE SHOWSTOPPER!

Chocolate cake was Quentin's favourite thing
to make in the whole world.

But as he carried his incredible
creation to the judging table . . .

WHOOOOO

He slipped!

CRASH went his chocolate creation.
And as for his disguise . . .

Oh dear.
Poor Quentin.

But then something very unexpected happened.

One little bunny
came over to help

and soon . . .

two, then three, then ALL the bunnies helped
put Quentin's cake together again.

The judges read out the final scores.

Quentin couldn't believe it.

He had won!
The Golden Egg Baker
of the Year trophy was his!

Quentin loved to bake.

His favourite was chocolate cake
and best of all,

it was somebody else's favourite too.